Little, Brown and Company

Hachette Book Group
1290 Avenue of the Americas, New York, NY 10104
Visit our website at lb-kids.com

LB kids is an imprint of Little, Brown and Company.
The LB kids name and logo are trademarks of Hachette Book Group, Inc.

The publisher is not responsible for websites (or their content) that are not owned by the publisher.

First Edition: September 2014

Library of Congress Control Number: 2013954888

ISBN 978-0-316-27704-4

10 9 8 7 6 5 4 3 2

CW

Printed in the United States of America

Licensed By:

TRANSFORMERS RESCUE BOTS

The Ghosts of Griffin Rock

Adapted by John Sazaklis
Based on the episode "The Haunting of Griffin Rock"
written by Steve Aranguren

LITTLE, BROWN & COMPANY
LB kids

It is a dark and stormy night. Jerry is driving an armored truck full of money down a winding road along the edge of a cliff. With a crash of thunder and a flash of lightning, the glowing figure of a woman appears!

While Chase and Chief Burns take the brothers back to jail, Kade turns to the others and says, "Looks like the hauntings were a hoax after all."

Suddenly, the Lady of Griffin Rock appears and cries, "Come home to me!"

Kade jumps with fright. "Was that a hologram or a ghost?!"

Cody smiles and says, "We'll never know!"

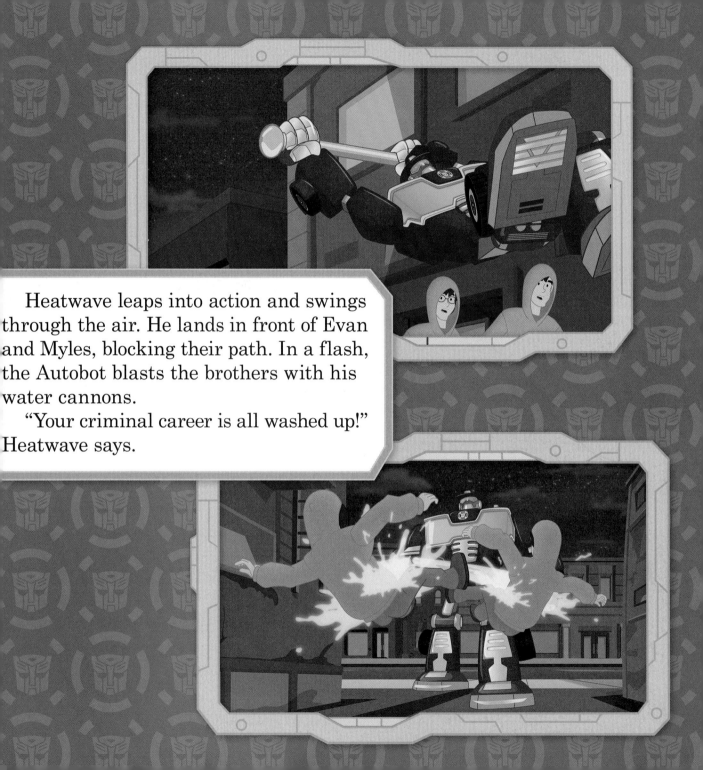

Heatwave leaps into action and swings through the air. He lands in front of Evan and Myles, blocking their path. In a flash, the Autobot blasts the brothers with his water cannons.

"Your criminal career is all washed up!" Heatwave says.

As Evan and Myles make their escape, they come face-to-face with the law.

"Halt, burglars," cries Chase. "We have you surrounded!"

But the brothers do not stop. They run through the legs of the robots as fast as they can.

Meanwhile, the two brothers are in the jewelry store filling up their burlap bags with expensive items.

"That police chief and his team of tin cans aren't as smart as we are." Evan laughs.

"Yeah," Myles agrees. "Thanks to our dirty little trick, we're picking this city clean."

Another alarm blares.

Now a jewelry store is the target. Chief Burns contacts his team and tells them where the burglars are striking.

"It's time to put an end to this ghost story!" he says.

The Rescue Bots roll out to the scene of the crime.

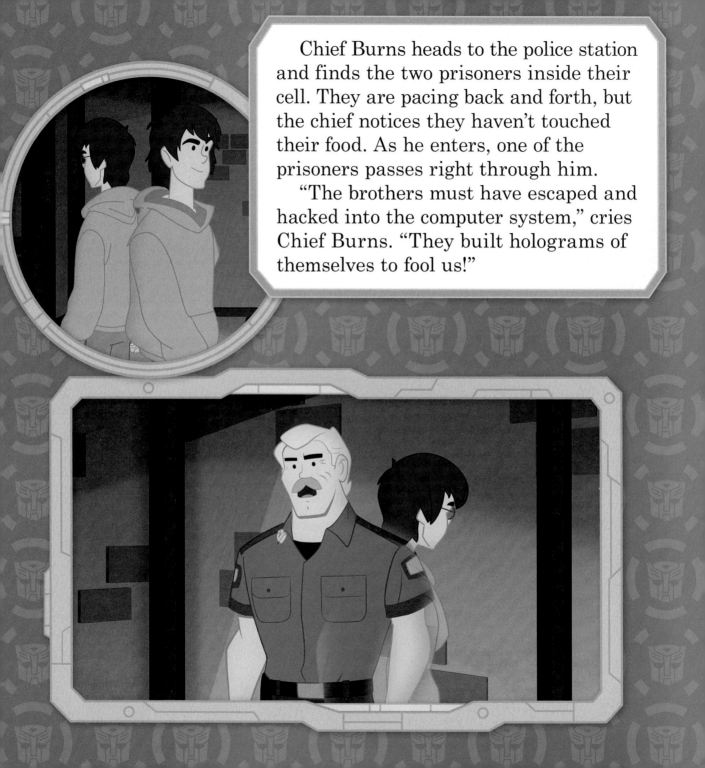

Chief Burns heads to the police station and finds the two prisoners inside their cell. They are pacing back and forth, but the chief notices they haven't touched their food. As he enters, one of the prisoners passes right through him.

"The brothers must have escaped and hacked into the computer system," cries Chief Burns. "They built holograms of themselves to fool us!"

The team goes to Doc Greene's lab. After some quick research, they learn that the holograms are coming from different projectors throughout the city.

"The signal is originating from the jail," the scientist says.

On the screen is an image of brothers Evan and Myles. "Ghosts can't steal," Cody says, "but those two do it for a living!"

"That ghost is toast!" Frankie cheers.

But the victory is short-lived because the ghost reappears.

"Hmm," says Doc Greene. "My readings show that this is not a ghost—it's a hologram!"

At that moment, Doc Greene arrives downtown with Cody and Frankie. "How do we stop the ghosts?" Graham asks.

"Allow me," Doc Greene replies. He pulls out his Spectral Vapor Filter and activates it. An energy field zaps one of the ghosts, causing it to fizzle and fade.

The firefighter and the Autobot enter the restaurant and make a discovery. "Fire's out, but the register has been robbed," Kade says into his Com-Link.

Heatwave and Kade rush to a restaurant that has gone up in flames.

"Finally," says Kade. "An emergency I know how to handle!"

Kade grabs a nearby hose and blasts the blaze until the fire is out.

Cody relays that there have been many more ghost sightings. Citizens are fleeing for their lives!

Chief Burns and the Rescue Bots are seeing ghosts, too, but they still can't believe their eyes!

Cody's voice crackles over the Com-Link. "Guys, there are a lot of weird calls coming in," he says.

"Tell me it's not another ghost," replies Dani.

"Okay," says Cody. "It's a whole *lot* of other ghosts!"

Chief Burns and his team race to the large vault. The contents have been completely cleared!

"How did that ghost empty the vault?" Boulder asks. "We were right behind it!"

"It didn't," answers the chief. "Ghosts can't steal."

The team deduces that the ghost was really a distraction, but they still don't know who, or what, the actual culprit is.

The ghost floats away from the bank and down an alley, with the rescue team in pursuit. And, just as swiftly, it passes through a brick wall. The heroes find themselves at a dead end. Suddenly, the bank alarm goes off.

"Everyone, back inside!" yells Chief Burns.

The Rescue Bots arrive at the bank. The lobby is empty.

"See? I told you," Kade says. "There's no such thing as ghosts. We're just wasting our time."

Suddenly, a specter materializes before them. "Follow me!" it beckons.

"After that phantom!" cries Chief Burns.

The next day, the emergency line rings. Chief Burns answers it, then says, "There's a ghost at the bank scaring away the customers."

The team exchanges concerned looks. Something spooky is happening in Griffin Rock.

"That's great!" Frankie exclaims. "It's the perfect opportunity to test my dad's Spectral Vapor Filters. They're designed to catch ghosts!"

"Rescue Bots," commands Heatwave, "roll to the rescue!"

Later that night, Cody tells Frankie about the rescue. "Who's the Lady of Griffin Rock?" he asks.

"Her name was Charlotte Wayne. Two hundred years ago, her husband and son were lost at sea," Frankie answers in a spooky voice. "Legend says that Charlotte's ghost is still looking for her family."

"Whoa." Cody gulps.

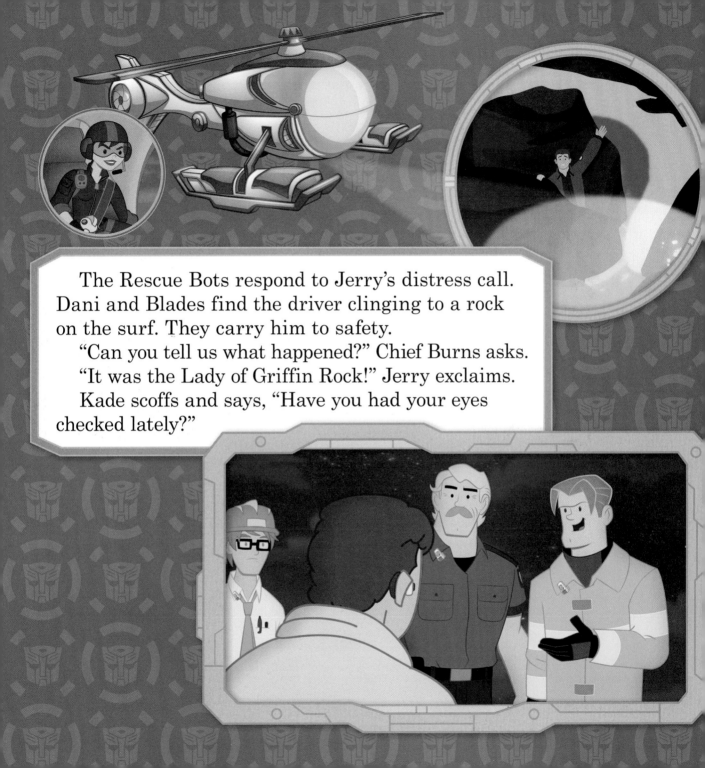

The Rescue Bots respond to Jerry's distress call. Dani and Blades find the driver clinging to a rock on the surf. They carry him to safety.

"Can you tell us what happened?" Chief Burns asks.

"It was the Lady of Griffin Rock!" Jerry exclaims.

Kade scoffs and says, "Have you had your eyes checked lately?"

She floats toward the truck and whispers in an eerie voice, "Come home to me...."

Scared, Jerry swerves, and the armored truck plows into a guardrail, flinging the driver into the water below.